This book is dedicated to our son, Elias David Talbert

Don't let anyone tell you it's too far to go,
Know that you're unstoppable,
'Cause the square root of what's possible is possible in YOU!

Loving you always and forever,
Mommy and Daddy

And to kids and kids at heart everywhere,
anything is possible if you just believe!

RAZORBILL

An imprint of Penguin Random House LLC, New York

First published in the United States of America by Razorbill, an imprint of Penguin Random House LLC, 2020

Visit us online at penguinrandomhouse.com.

Library of Congress Cataloging-in-Publication Data is available.

ISBN 9780593203835

Printed in the United States of America

1 3 5 7 9 10 8 6 4 2

Design by Kristin Boyle & Maria Fazio
Text set in Sabon LT Std

THE SQUARE ROOT OF POSSIBLE

A JINGLE JANGLE STORY

LYN SISSON-TALBERT & DAVID E. TALBERT

ILLUSTRATED BY TARA NICOLE WHITAKER

RAZORBILL

Journey loved to make things. She liked to tinker, to engineer, to invent.

When she was hard at work, puzzling her way from a pile of parts to a brand-new creation, Journey saw things—beautiful things.

Formulas, equations. Numbers, logic, paths from here to there. From start to finish. From problem to solution.

Journey saw things that shouldn't be possible. She made things that shouldn't be possible.

But because Journey believed in them—they were.

It's a wonderful thing,
to see impossible things.
To have extraordinary vision.

But it can be lonely, too,
when people don't see what you see.

"You get it from your grandfather," Journey's mom said with a funny smile.

Journey had never met her grandfather. All she knew was:

What I Know about Grandpa

1. his name is Jeronicus Jangle

2. he lives far away

3. he was the greatest inventor of all time!

"He used to make the most marvelous toys and inventions," Journey's mom said.

She always looked a little sad when she talked about her father, Jeronicus, but proud too.

Journey wanted to meet her grandfather. She wanted to meet
someone who was like her—who saw the things she saw. She wanted
to work side by side with the great inventor Jeronicus Jangle.

And so Journey set off to Cobbleton.

But when Journey found her grandfather, there were no glowing formulas. There were no dancing numbers. There weren't even any tools. Or materials. Or notebooks filled with scribbled notes.

There was just a grouchy old man who didn't seem very happy to see Journey.

This was a problem for sure, but Journey loved problems. Finding the solution was always so satisfying.

Jeronicus Jangle had lost his jingle, and Journey was going to help him get it back.

Journey's grouchy grandfather was poking at something interesting. It didn't look like it was going so well, so Journey decided to help.

She scribbled a glowing formula into the air. Words and numbers, truth and magic. Time. Chance. Belief.

"You can see that?" her grandfather said.

"Can't you?" asked Journey.

Her grandfather looked glum. "No," he said. "Not anymore."

Journey stayed up late that night, thinking about the square root of possible.

There was a variable missing from her grandfather's life. His crankiness had been multiplied by boredom, which was bad enough. But the long division of lonely . . . that was the real problem.

What Jeronicus Jangle was missing was *Fun*.
Fun would balance that equation.
Fun canceled out bitterness. Fun subtracted sadness.

In the morning, a fresh coat of snow blanketed Cobbleton. It was beautiful. And more than that . . . Journey happened to know what snow added up to . . .

Journey knew just what she needed to do.

Splat!

Her snowball socked Jeronicus right on the head.
Journey giggled. Bull's-eye!

For one terrible moment, Jeronicus Jangle looked grouchier than ever.

Come on! Journey thought. *The square root of possible and the fourth snowball theorem dictates an equal and opposite reaction! So, react!*

And then . . .

He began scribbling furiously in the snow. At first, the symbols only glowed faintly. But as Journey's grandfather built a fearsome new formula, the letters and numbers began to burn in the air.

Nobody but Journey and Jeronicus could see them.

Nobody but Journey and Jeronicus believed in them.

But that didn't mean they weren't real. They were the realest thing ever.

Powered by the pure math of mischief, the snowball whizzed through the crowd. It swerved around corners. It hopped over lampposts. Journey dodged and ducked, but the snowball had a vision.

Splat!

Journey had never been so happy to get a face full of
snow in her whole life.

It was the most magnificent mathematical snowball fight Cobbleton had ever seen.

And the best part of all of it was that her square root of possible theorem worked!

Fun minus sad . . .
     . . . multiplied by mischief . . .
          . . . divided by love . . .
               . . . with the addition of affection added for good measure . . .

equals Joy!

The Square Root of Possible

Where's the world that you created
And the stories that you painted
With words that made me feel ten feet tall
Where's the magic in the moonlight
The surprise hidden in plain sight
No, I don't see much
To inspire much
At all
And I'm ready now
To fly away
And gravity won't get a thing to say
It's my choice if I get to touch the sky
Is it possible that the square root of impossible is me
It's so possible
Watch me rise high above my obstacles
Watch me become who I'm supposed to be
Oh the possibilities
'Cause the square root of impossible is possible
In me
In me